The True Story
of the
Three Billy Goats Gruff:
The Troll's Side
of the Story

Written by David Reynolds
Illustrated by Myles Reichel

THE TRUE STORY OF THE THREE BILLY GOATS GRUFF:
THE TROLL'S SIDE OF THE STORY
Written by David Reynolds
Illustrated by Myles Reichel

This edition also features Sir George Webbe Dasent's 1859 translation of "The Three Billy Goats Gruff."

ISBN-13: 978-0-9869027-4-1

Published by Problematic Press.

To purchase copies of this book, please visit: http://problematicpress.wordpress.com

Printed in the United States.

Cover art by Myles Reichel.

The hat logo is a trademark of Problematic Press.

Table of Contents

To my parents and sisters, who read with me endlessly when I was young. Thank you to no end. To the teacher who prompted this story in class and the one who selected it for publication in *Chalkdust and Chewing Gum* (Jesperson Press, 1992). I bet ye had no idea what literary monster ye had unleashed. My thanks to ye both, too. And, for all the children and children-at-heart, please, read and enjoy!

    – David Reynolds

For all my family that are my friends, and all my friends that are my family. I couldn't have chosen better. The love and support for everything I do is more than I could ever ask for. To those who encouraged me to pursue my passions, I owe you more than I can ever repay. For you who have had an effect on my life, however big or small, thank you. This one is for you. May our paths cross again.

    – Myles Reichel

Introduction

The tale told here was written by a young David Reynolds, when the author was just about 9-11 years old. It was originally written as an assignment for school, but it was later selected to be published, along with many other children's works, in a collection called *Chalkdust and Chewing Gum* (Jesperson Press, 1992). Also featured in this edition is a translation of the classic folktale by Sir George Webbe Dasent as it appeared in *Popular Tales from the Norse* (1859). This provides the perfect juxtaposition for the two tales.

Having re-discovered this little gem, Reynolds thought it held a certain charm and so he decided to publish it independently, but with illustrations this time. Partnering with long-time friend Myles Reichel, the two developed the book you hold in your hands. Reichel's illustrations have given this tale a new vibrance and life. The bulk of the tale remains as it was written by young Reynolds, with the exception of the final lines. An older Reynolds thought these should be added, just to provide some closure.

Please, read and enjoy!

THE THREE BILLY GOATS GRUFF

Once on a time there were three billy goats, who were to go up to the hill-side to make themselves fat, and the name of all three was "Gruff."

On the way up was a bridge over a burn they had to cross; and under the bridge lived a great ugly Troll, with eyes as big as saucers, and a nose as long as a poker.

So first of all came the youngest billy goat Gruff to cross the bridge.

"Trip, trap; trip, trap!" went the bridge.

"WHO"S THAT tripping over my bridge?" roared the Troll.

"Oh! it is only I, the tiniest billy goat Gruff; and I'm going up to the hill-side to make myself fat," said the billy goat, with such a small voice.

"Now, I'm coming to gobble you up," said the Troll.

"Oh, no! pray don"t take me. I'm too little, that I am", said the billy goat; "wait a bit until the second billy goat Gruff comes, he's much bigger."

"Well! be off with you," said the Troll.

A little while after came the second billy goat Gruff to cross the bridge.

"TRIP, TRAP! TRIP, TRAP! TRIP, TRAP!" went the bridge.

"WHO'S THAT tripping over my bridge?" roared the Troll.

"Oh! it's the second billy goat Gruff, and I'm going up to the hill-side to make myself fat," said the billy goat, who hadn't such a small voice.

"Now, I'm coming to gobble you up," said the Troll.

"Oh, no! don't take me, wait a little till the big billy goat Gruff comes, he's much bigger."

"Very well! Be off with you," said the Troll.

But just then up came the big billy goat Gruff.

"TRIP, TRAP! TRIP, TRAP! TRIP, TRAP!" went the bridge, for the billy goat was so heavy that the bridge creaked and groaned under him.

"WHO'S THAT tramping over my bridge?" roared the Troll.

"IT'S I! THE BIG billy goat GRUFF," said the billy goat, who had an ugly hoarse voice of his own.

"Now, I'm coming to gobble you up," roared the Troll.

"Well, come along! I've got two spears,
And I'll poke your eyeballs out at your ears;
I've got besides two curling-stones,
And I'll crush you to bits, body and bones."

That was what the big billy goat said; and so he flew at the Troll and poked his eyes out with his horns, and crushed him to bits, body and bones, and tossed him out into the burn, and after that he went up to the hill-side. There the billy goats got so fat they were scarce able to walk home again; and if the fat hasn't fallen off them, why they're still fat; and so:

Snip, snap, snout,
This tale's told out.

... or, is it?

The True Story

of the

Three Billy Goats Gruff:

The Troll's Side

of the Story

One spring morning on my vacation, I was resting under the bridge.

Then I heard someone come near the bridge. Whoever it was he was tramping very hard.

I went on top of the bridge to see who it was. It was the youngest billy goat Gruff.

The Gruffs are very weird.
He saw me and jumped over the
side of the bridge with fright.

"Hey, that must be lies they say about you being mean," said the billy goat.

"Yeah. I really love animals," I said. "You can go now, if you want to," and I went back under the bridge.

Then I heard wheels.
It was the teenage Gruff
on a skateboard.

He hit a rock and went flying over the side of the bridge.

The oldest billy goat saw me and he thought I was trying to drown his little brother.

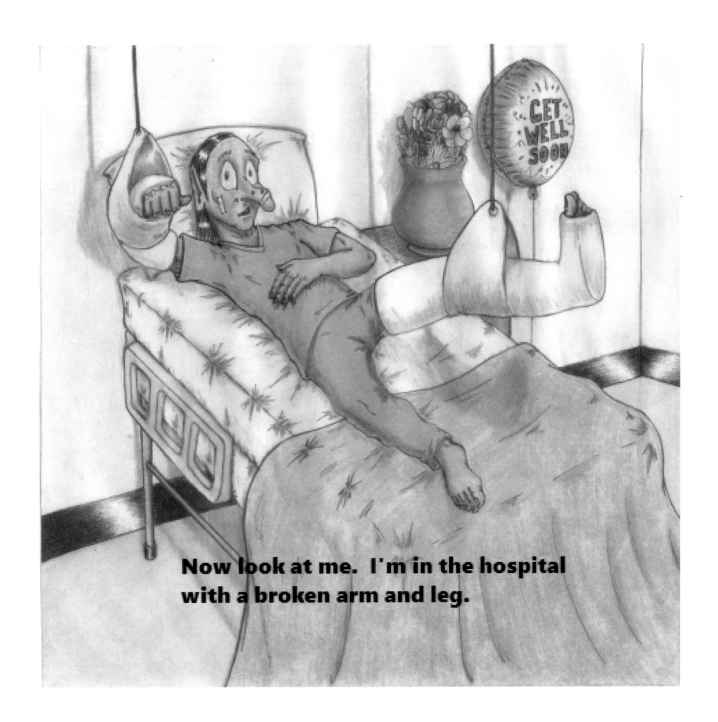

Now look at me. I'm in the hospital with a broken arm and leg.

But, don't be sad now, for troll's are tough. This one healed real quick, and he returned to his bridge before long.

Problematic Press is a small, independent book publishing endeavour based in St. John's, NL. Problematic Press has a mission with a broad scope, aiming to entertain and educate readers of all ages.

Perhaps that's problematic. Problems make us think.

http://problematicpress.wordpress.com

Made in the USA
Charleston, SC
26 April 2014